KNOTTY & ICE

AN EVE OF LIGHT SHORT STORY

HARAMBEE K. GREY-SUN

HYPERVERSE BOOKS, LLC

Copyright © 2014, 2020 by Harambee K. Grey-Sun

Cover design by James, GoOnWrite.com.

ISBN-13: 978-1-64044-901-5

Published by **HyperVerse Books, LLC**

www.hyperversebooks.com

writing between and beyond the lines

KNOTTY & ICE

Neal didn't stop for the cyclist. He didn't even take the time to consider himself lucky when the kid swerved out of his Acura's path.

On a mission, he took up two spaces in the parking lot then almost forgot to lock the car's doors as he dashed for the convenience store's entrance. He hustled up and down the aisles twice before finally losing it.

"*Dammit*—Don't you have any Listerine?"

"Sorry, shiny," the clerk hollered back at him.

Neal knew his skin was still covered in baby oil—only in the car did he realize it might've been wise to rinse off before he'd left Lady Kat's room—but the fact the clerk could tell he was slicked up from a couple dozen feet away only made him more anxious. What if the chuckling fool made a leap in logic and figured it out? Shiny head and arms sticking out of a wrinkled, stained polo . . . Couldn't have been the worst or oddest of what has passed through the convenience store; but the clerk wouldn't take his eyes off him.

"We have a dry mouth oral rinse." The fool, still chuckling, may or may not have been trying to be helpful.

"I need something that kills odors," Neal said. "*Germs.*"

"It does the same thing."

"No, it *doesn't.*"

He had to get out of there. He had to get out of the store, and out of the area. He wanted to just go and jump in some magic acid bath, something that would cleanse and purify his clothes and body, inside and out.

He grabbed the bottle of oral rinse and laid three dollars on the counter.

"One short, dude," the clerk said.

"It's only a three-ounce bot—" Neal closed his eyes and sighed. "Never mind." He gave the clerk another buck and twisted off the cap as he headed for the exit. For the next ten minutes, he stood next to his car, swishing, sloshing, and gargling the bottle's contents. It was no use. He couldn't wash the taste from his mouth. Or the stench from his upper lip.

He got into his Acura and sped off. He'd take the back roads, making sure he reached the Agency even faster than if he'd taken the highway. He sure as hell could maneuver a vehicle more smoothly and successfully than he could a woman's body. His experience with the Kat had certainly confirmed that.

She was in-call only, just as Neal preferred. And there was a fifteen-year age difference, also as he preferred (he was too embarrassed to be with anyone near his own age). A different ethnicity? Check. She wasn't anything close to Irish, not even a so-called Black Irish like himself. And he'd stuck to his aliases—"NumberJuan" on email and cell, and "Juan" in person. Everything was working, except for the one thing that never really worked.

He wasn't a virgin. He was something worse. *Inept*. He couldn't hold a girlfriend because he had no technique. Sloppy kisses and awkward caresses had yet to impress any. He did have what he once thought of as a secret weapon, over eight inches long. But it didn't take long for him to recognize that wasn't enough. *It's not the size that counts; it's what you do with it.* His sexual adulthood had been a progression from wet-noodle wielder to—with the assistance of a little yellow pill—cannon carrier, one that refused to fire when he was with a partner (though he did just fine on his own).

His lifelong dream of having a child was fading with each passing day. Thirty-five years out of his mother's womb and he still was no closer to being able to sow his own seed, not for the lack of trying. After thirty minutes of fumbling around with a woman, unable to even come close to ejaculating, his interest in satisfying her steeply declined. Frustration was a mood-killer no drug could reverse.

When his partners' reactions passed from "That's okay, baby" through yawning to "What the fuck . . . Are you gay?" he decided he needed practice. He bought a red smartphone and a new account to match; then he hit the backpages. He scheduled appointments with escorts who operated far from his neighborhood and his other regular haunts, but not *too* far. A Heartland Security agent using most of his personal time to make long-distance trips would quickly raise suspicion and potentially call down the wrath of superiors.

He'd been successfully elusive for six months now. But practice wasn't making perfect; it was just making him sick.

Fifty years old and heavyset, Lady Kat initially seemed promising. She'd agreed to meet him in her motel room on Saturday morning, 11:00, roughly two hours before he'd have to head in for his shift. Neal performed his usual surveillance ahead of time. As a member of the Agency's elite Peacemakers, a special-mission unit, he damn sure knew how to stay invisible while scouting territory, ensuring it was safe to enter. He'd perfected that skill, at least. Good thing the Heartland Security Agency was interested in hiring Peacemakers rather than Lovemakers.

Lady Kat was big, but voluptuous. A pleasing smile and gorgeous eyes that seemed to shift back and forth between green and blue both relaxed and aroused him. The body-rub he'd explicitly come for went well enough, even if her palms felt like she'd been laying brick with her bare hands. After she disrobed and they began entangling for what he'd implicitly come for, things went downhill—in more ways than one. He kissed her on the forehead and steadily made his way south. Her skin was sticky but tasty, as if she'd used maple syrup for lotion, but her thong, the one piece of clothing she'd kept on, smelled like the kitchen of a fast burger joint and had the greasy taste to match. He made sure the thong stayed on, and he stayed away from the patch for the rest of the hour.

He'd left the room with a mild feeling of nausea and something verging on a migraine, but the lingering odor in his nostrils and film on his tongue were what he most wanted to rid himself of before arriving at work. He could take a shower once he got there.

He couldn't help but appear as a heap of something one would wisely steer clear of if one spotted it in one's path. And most of his coworkers were wise. Unfortunately for his unit partner, she had no choice but to get close.

"You're almost late," Katrisha said.

"Almost." Neal dropped his bag in his chair and rummaged through his desk drawers.

"Why are you so shiny?" she asked.

He answered with a more important question. "Do you have any mouthwash?"

Katrisha sniffed. "Is that coconut oil?"

"Like *strong* mouthwash?" Neal repeated.

She shook her head. "Why didn't you get some on the way in?"

He smirked as he pulled his toothbrush out of the drawer. "Because I was almost late."

Katrisha shifted her eyes downward and nodded. "How'd you know? You're not wearing your watch."

Neal followed her eyes and dropped his brush. "Shit . . . Oh *shit!*"

The watch was Agency-issue, a prototype of a device developed in conjunction, and in *secret*, with a private contractor. As Neal understood it, the device was designed to connect with the nervous system and somehow enhance the body's electrical activity to the point where the air around the skin, the tiniest fraction of an inch, acted as a force field of some kind; they were experimenting with watches before they moved on to neural implants. Neal and other select Peacemakers were to wear the devices out in the field, testing them in action so they could be studied and improved. They looked like normal digital watches, almost exactly like Neal's old one, so he thought nothing of taking it off with the rest of his clothes and laying it on Lady Kat's nightstand. When it came time to leave, he was far more worried about getting the hell out of there without vomiting.

"Go back home and *get* it." Katrisha usually wasn't one to get emotional. She was professional through and through, believing wholeheartedly in the Agency's mission and following orders without question. What he saw in her eyes now was fiery intensity, so much of it her irises seemed to glow. Even though Neal was her senior in the unit, and her mentor, he'd screwed up, and she wasn't going to stand for it.

"It's not at home."

"Where is it?"

"It's . . . not at home." He wasn't sure what to say. Several years back, in the aftermath of President Sullivan cheating on his wife and being murdered for it, the law euphemistically dubbed the "Mistress Act" made prostitution and other pay-to-play sexual activities a severe crime, punishable by a minimum three-year prison sentence. One strike and you're in. To survive as an escort these days, one had to be smart and discreet: accept cash only, and for companionship only; the word "sex" and common terms for sexual activities were never to be mentioned in an escort's presence, not even in private settings. Not all those who advertised in the backpages knew the unspoken rules. Neal knew to only pick those who'd been advertising for some time; they were the ones who best knew how to stay out of jail and protect their clients. Now, he felt as naked as he'd actually been in Lady Kat's den.

"Neal, you need to get that watch back. If it—"

"Falls into the wrong hands—I know, I know." He waved her off as he hustled toward the stairs and pulled out his red smartphone. He wasn't about to risk a call. Even a text was too chancy within a building housing those dedicated to surveillance and security. He did send Kat a brief, cryptic email while making his way to the parking garage. He didn't expect a reply before he got back to the motel, but he wanted to try to give her a head's up he was coming.

He unlocked his Acura.

"We're taking the SUV."

"The fu—" Neal almost dropped his phone at the sound of Katrisha's voice. "Were you *following* me?"

"We're on Agency time now. Neither of us is off duty. Wherever you're going, I'm going."

Neal muttered three obscenities before following his partner to the black armored vehicle. Katrisha settled herself in the driver's seat as she asked, "So, we're not going to your place?"

"Just get us out of the garage," Neal said. "I'll guide you."

She drove the speed limit, but it still seemed a little too fast for him. Maybe because his brain had slowed down, inversely proportionate to the millions of rapid thoughts he'd had after seeing his bare wrist.

"What did you do this morning?"

Katrisha's question was a casual attempt at small talk, but in his ears the words were the drip-drop beginning of an interrogation.

"I had brunch," he said after a moment.

"On Saturday?" she asked. "Who around here serves brunch on Saturdays?"

"Someone who shouldn't."

The vehicle was silent until they crossed the city line, officially exiting Indianapolis. Katrisha sped up, edging over the limit.

"Where?"

Neal sighed. "The Perfection Inn. About two miles down."

They parked in the guests' section. Neal unbuckled and held up his hand as Katrisha opened her door.

"Would you mind letting me check this out alone?" he asked.

She furrowed her brow.

"Just stay here and call in," he said. "See where we're supposed to go next."

She seemed content with this, softening her eyes as she closed her door. Neal got out and ran, rounded a corner, then banged on door 204. After a minute of silence, he banged again. He dialed the Lady on his red smartphone. No answer. And still no response to his earlier email.

To hell with this. He tried to hear through the windows and peer through the drawn curtains. It was possible she was with her next appointment, but Neal was beyond caring—and he didn't have time to go to the motel manager with an explanation (even a false one) and request a key. His reputation, job, and freedom were on the line. Such a sudden realization could really push a man.

He drew his Glock and fired at the window. He was built like a running back, but he had no hope of breaking down a deadbolted door without injuring himself. The window was safer—for him, if not for whomever was on the other side.

He kicked in most of the glass, brushed aside the curtains, and crawled through. There was no trace of the Kat. No clothes, no toiletries, no odors . . . and no watch. The room was clean. The woman must've checked out right after Neal had left.

This time, before he could leave, his partner, someone who was probably the motel manager, and several onlookers gathered at the broken window and now-open door. Neal took a deep breath and calmly held up his HSA badge. The onlookers scattered. The manager backed away from the door. When Katrisha cleared her throat and flashed her badge, the manager glanced and scrambled away.

People, particularly people in the Midwest, knew why the HSA had been founded. Most folks harboring memories of immoral deeds shied away from the agents, lest they end up *disappeared*. Of course, that was just an urban legend among Middle Americans. If one cheated on his wife with a married woman, or had sex with a child, HSA agents wouldn't just drop out of the blue and throw the offender into a black hole. The offender would get a trial first.

Neal was getting the first taste of his trial now.

"What the hell is going on, Neal?" Katrisha stood in the doorway, glaring again with the fire in her eyes. This time, it was less a poetic impression; he actually thought her eyes flickered.

"Let's talk in the car." He walked toward it. "You called in to the Agency?"

Katrisha nodded.

"What'd they say?"

"Get back to the Agency."

They said nothing more until Katrisha had put several miles between them and the motel. She wasn't going to repeat her earlier question; she apparently felt she'd said enough. She was a good agent. She knew how and when to apply the silent treatment on one with a damaged conscience.

"I . . ." Neal cleared his throat. "I was with a woman this morning. I left the watch on the nightstand. An accident."

"Could be more serious than that," Katrisha said quietly, "depending on what she does with it."

Neal gazed through the windshield, looking at nothing.

"What type of woman was she?" Katrisha asked. "Young? In her twenties? What color were her nails? How was her hair styled?" She asked three questions in the amount of time it took Neal to answer one. She was the sharpest mentee he'd ever had. A description of the woman—everything from her appearance, age, and the way that she spoke—could help them narrow down the type of people with whom Lady Kat might run around, and the type of locales she might frequent. But when Neal gave Katrisha the Lady's age and appearance, the junior agent seemed stumped. Escorts of this type were rare; most either were or tried to pass themselves off as twenty- or thirty-something models.

"She probably operates alone," Katrisha said, "or with a single partner. A boyfriend, or a permissive husband."

Neal was shocked that Katrisha had remained so professional after his admission. Maybe she just wanted to do her duty for the day—retrieve the watch—before shepherding his termination and imprisonment.

"Whores like that . . ." Katrisha mused. "She's probably a swinger."

Neal's red phone buzzed. He'd received a text.

U want me? Ow!

It was Lady Kat. Neal texted back, responding with the obvious question. He received a less obvious answer.

Meat 2nite at SXS. 9:30.

"What are you doing?" Katrisha asked.

"SXS." He ignored her sharp tone. "You know what that is?"

"It's a swinger's club on—" She paused before shifting her tone again. "Is that that bitch? Hand me your phone!"

"Just keep driving," Neal said.

"Hand me your phone! I can trace—"

"Keep *both* hands on the wheel," Neal said. "She's already switched phones. I only know it's her because she included some stupid puns in her messages. She'll switch again before you or I can do anything."

"She's at the SXS? Let's go."

"*No.* She said 9:30. She wouldn't have given us a location if she were there already." Lady Kat was going to be more trouble than he thought. Swinger, escort, whatever—she was starting a dangerous game. For the first time, Neal considered whether she probably—somehow—had targeted him, possibly just to get the watch.

"So we're just going back to headquarters to twiddle our thumbs till then?"

"We're going to get backup," Neal said, "and to strategize. I have the feeling she's not all we're going to have to deal with tonight."

Katrisha mumbled something.

"How did you know, just off the top of your head, SXS was a swinger's club?" he asked.

"It's my job to know. It's *our* job."

Neal stayed silent for the rest of the drive.

RUFUS, the head of Indiana's Peacemaker unit, appropriately and sufficiently chewed Neal out before allowing him to shower and change into his uniform.

The HSA had only one local branch in the state of Indiana. Ohio and Illinois both got two, while Michigan and Kentucky both had only one. Neal and his colleagues had spent countless hours discussing Washington's bias and debating whether Indiana could use one more office, say in Gary, or even in Evansville. But today he experienced a big benefit of working in a state's sole office: the top men more jealously guarded their own, happily ignoring protocol when it came to some of their best and more senior employees. Some of that had to do with a we-need-all-the-help-we-can-get mentality. But much of it had to do with turning a blind eye to stupid, minor crimes to focus on the perpetrators of bigger ones.

Neal was reprimanded but he'd keep his job, and take a slight reduction in pay—roughly the amount he'd probably spend on escorts over a six-month period. He considered that fair enough. The memory of his most recent wasn't going away any time soon.

Neither was the oil. He spent fifteen minutes in the shower to no benefit. Whatever it was, it certainly wasn't baby oil. He grumbled to himself as he dressed, mixing curses with vows to pick up stronger soap after work. He then hurried on to the planning room.

There were a dozen Peacemakers already waiting; that was half the number in the entire office. Katrisha, sitting up front, motioned for Neal to join her. Rufus then stood and explained the mission, gave some background about the club and its neighborhood, then asked Katrisha to take over. Before she could even stand and speak, she was hit with a question.

"Is it really going to require all of us?" one of the Peacemakers asked. "Can't three or four of us just go in undercover?"

"Two of us should go in undercover," Katrisha said, "me and Neal. Any more than that is too risky. But we'll need backup at every entrance and potential exit."

"For what?" another Peacemaker asked. "We're talking about perverts, here, not gangsters."

Katrisha and Rufus exchanged glances before the latter said, "You all know about the White Fire Virus. You've been briefed many times on what some of its carriers can do. You're damn right we're going into a den of sexual perverts, one or more of whom will likely be infected with the STD."

"Why else would this woman hole up there and send us an invitation?" Katrisha said.

Neal bowed his head. When he began his practice sessions with escorts, he did consider STDs. He'd always worn a condom, but even a child knew rubbers didn't offer 100% protection. If Lady Kat had not just an STD but the strangest and most feared one of all . . .

What the hell had he done to earn this rotten spot?

"Neal will provide us with a description," Katrisha said. "I just want to say, don't trust your eyes. Anything that looks like . . . whatever—ghost, demon, or angel—*shoot* it. Multiple times. Washington won't let us quarantine these plague carriers, but . . . Well, use your best judgment, the judgment we've been trained to use."

Neal heaved his shoulders and sighed as the savvy agent retook her seat. It appeared the mentee was quickly surpassing the mentor on the levels of respect.

He stood and described everything about Lady Kat he could remember—how she looked, sounded, and smelled (eliciting chuckles), what she'd been wearing, and everything she'd told him during their moment by candlelight. He wasn't sure how this was helpful for the mission; part of him just wanted to confess as a way of absolving himself. Another part of him dwelled on the fact he was destined to live his life childless, having accomplished nothing meaningful outside of his low-paying job. Nothing beyond close friendships was in his future. And if he'd somehow contracted the Virus, a much worse fate would welcome him.

THE SXS WAS AS PACKED as expected for a Saturday night, and no one gave Neal or Katrisha any kind of hassle as they paid the cover and headed toward the bar. It helped immensely that Peacemaker uniforms were nothing like military or police uniforms. They came in a variety of colors and designs, were armored in the right places, stocked with hidden (and dangerous) goodies, and yet they were fashionable enough to wear among the urban public without raising suspicion. The style changed every so often to help prevent Peacemakers from being made. So far on this night, the uniforms were working like a charm.

The downstairs bar had about twenty stools; there were also a few booths and tables where folks could drink and chat; but the doors lining the walls were the main feature of the club. Once they became acquainted out in the open, couples, threesomes, foursomes, and whatever else were expected to go behind closed doors to fulfill their seductive promises. Ostensibly no money changed hands between partners, and no one was actually cheating, so whatever took place behind closed doors was perfectly legal. Neal guessed the second floor had at least twice the number of rooms.

He wasn't surprised such a place would draw such a large crowd. In today's society, it seemed more and more people were hooking up any way that they could and as often as they could, maybe—at least subconsciously—as some form of protest. Or maybe sex performed properly allowed its participants to achieve an ecstasy no drug could deliver. He could only speculate. Perhaps there wasn't much going on in their minds at all. Some of them may've simply viewed all potential partners as shiny packages under a Christmas tree, something to be obtained, unwrapped, and enjoyed for a few hours, then pushed aside under the couch or into the closet after boredom set in.

Such a thought couldn't help but creep into Neal's mind as they reached the bar. No sooner had they sat down when a man with an open shirt and hairy chest took the stool on Katrisha's other side.

"From the moment you walked through the door, I couldn't take my eyes off you." The gigolo managed to speak both loudly and clearly while somehow maintaining a toothy grin. "Want to tell me what makes you so beautiful?"

Katrisha faced him and seemed to say, "I have one billion parasites living in my skin and blood. They do all the hard work."

Neal wasn't sure what he'd heard, but he saw the gigolo's face contort into an anguished grimace as it seemed to reflect a greenish pale light. The man fell off his stool, landed on his arm, and then scrambled away, rubbing his arm while glancing over his shoulder, as if hoping Katrisha wasn't following him.

Neal shook his head. "What happened?"

Katrisha turned toward him and grinned. "Guess he got the wrong impression."

There was something in her eyes—a twinkle—as if tiny stars or gems were buried at the center of their globes. She shivered slightly then turned away, motioning for the bartender.

"What'll you have?"

"Information." Katrisha laid her badge on the bar and a hundred-dollar bill next to it. "Looking for Lady Kat."

The bartender eyed the bill, then Katrisha, then the bill again. He edged his fingers toward the money. Katrisha put her hand on top.

"We already know she's here. Fifty bucks is for you to

tell us which room, and the other fifty is for telling us who she's with."

The bartender looked everywhere but at Katrisha, trying to figure who else was watching, or listening, before he leaned in. "She keeps a private room on the second floor. Number 42. She has a boyfriend. Acts as a bouncer in case her visitors get out of hand. He's here, but I don't know where."

"Just one guy?" Neal asked. "You sure?"

The bartender nodded.

"I'm sure," Katrisha said. "Their kind works in pairs." She released the hundred and said to the bartender, "More where that came from if you don't raise any alarms." He nodded again. She then turned to Neal. "I did my bit. You should probably lead from here."

Neal sighed and headed toward the staircase, ignoring every male, female, and whatever that smiled, winked, or tried to pull him aside. It wasn't hard to find room 42. It was almost directly opposite the stairs, and it had more space between it and its adjacent doors than most of the other rooms.

"I'll post by the door." Katrisha put her hand on one of her concealed weapons as she surveyed their surroundings, eyeballing potential hostiles, sizing them up, undoubtedly figuring which ones she could take out alone. It was what Neal normally would have done, but he was focused on the door. The hair on his arms and the back of his neck straightened. The day had turned increasingly complicated as it had progressed. Earlier, he was more than ready to storm Lady Kat's room, but now he felt he'd need protection—protection that Katrisha and the Peacemakers outside couldn't provide.

He knocked.

He barely heard the response over the noise behind him, but he swore it was a younger voice, sultrier than the one belonging to the woman he'd met that morning.

He entered.

His eyes immediately went to the St. Andrews cross and stayed there for a moment before moving on to the swings, the medical table, and the innumerable straps, canes, floggers, and other devices hanging from the wall. Under crimson lights, suffused with a New Age music that hadn't yet come of age, the room was a dungeon. His eyes drifted back to the cross.

"Did you come to play, or to pray?"

The Lady emerged from the shadows in the back of the long room, carrying a riding crop. Lady . . . or Mistress. Wearing a leather bustier and knee-high stiletto boots, the young woman seemed amused at his bewilderment.

His ears hadn't deceived him. This was not the woman he'd met with earlier. And, yet, it somehow was. She had the body and face of an athletic thirty-year-old. Her skin was darker, more dark chocolate than caramel. But those eyes . . . They glowed, unmistakably shifting between green and blue like malfunctioning traffic lights.

Neal swallowed. "I'm here for what's mine."

"Why don't you have a seat on the spanking bench, NumberJuan? I can give you everything you have coming." She approached, smiling and smacking the crop against her own bottom.

Neal's hand hovered near his concealed Glock.

"You're different," he said, "but I know you're you . . . Kat. I won't ask how, or why. Just give me the watch I left behind, and I'll leave you alone."

"Alone? Like you're destined to be?" She walked along the wall, fingering the various instruments and toys, reminiscing in a tone of false-fondness about their encounter that morning and all his inadequacies.

He'd been shirking lately, but he was still a seasoned agent. He knew what she was doing. He drew his gun. Before he could point it at her, Lady Kat grabbed two long, sharp, and pointy toys off the wall and came at him in a whirlwind.

She cut, sliced, slapped, and ducked—avoiding every offensive move, evading every defensive move—as she disarmed and rendered him naked in less than two minutes.

Neal was too thunderstruck to call for help, too shocked to retrieve one of his weapons, all of them now exposed at his feet. He only stood naked as he gazed at the grinning Lady.

"Still all slicked up, I see."

He glanced at his skin. His body glistened.

"What did you do to me?" he asked.

"I've begun to free you to be *you*." The Lady leapt at him, planting the stilettos under his chest and her hands around his neck before slipping him like a wet bar of soap and flipping him several feet backward. Neal braced himself for impact, but he never hit the floor.

The Lady had moved as if she were in a gyroscope, flipping and spinning around to catch him in a web of light cast by her fingertips. Neal's body splayed as if on the St. Andrew's cross, but he was in midair, gazing at the threads, each of them interwoven with black-and-crimson striped light and interspersed with glowing golden beads, all of it emanating from her skin and piercing his, simultaneously *stretching* and *tightening* his. He winced and grunted.

"Among its other benefits," Lady Kat said, "the oil will ensure this doesn't hurt nearly as much as it should."

"What . . . are you—" He sucked air through clenched

teeth. The threads felt like tweezers digging into his skin for loose filaments and tugging when finding them.

"I'm just working out the kinks," she said. "Showing you the relationship between *pain* and pleasure. The grotesque and the *beautiful*. The *true* relationship between us—the deviants, the perverts, the sexually dysfunctional—and this world of false appearances."

It felt to Neal as if every inch of his body had sprouted its own tiny tongue and each was being forced to lick a nine-volt battery.

"We're not to be shamed, or mocked, or pitied," Lady Kat said. "We're to recognize our chosen status and band together to destroy the *One*. The One who put us in this state, making us constantly think there was something wrong with us, making us live a life of constant psychological and physical torment. We'll turn that torment into eternal ecstasy and *kill* our Creator. We start with ourselves, preparing for the session to end all sessions by freezing the body, then setting the soul on fire."

His peals of screams didn't begin to express what he felt. But they were enough to bring a rescuer. Katrisha rushed through the door, gun ready, and fired at the Lady. Neal had never known her to miss, especially at such a close range, but the shots may as well have been warnings. The Lady barely shifted a shoulder as the bullets plugged the walls.

"Ice!"

Neal assumed her cry was some kind of snarky dis to Katrisha, but he soon realized that the Lady was calling for her own backup. A coal-black man the size of a riding mower and wearing nothing but a thong came barreling from the back of the room. Katrisha aimed her gun, but the man embraced her before she could get off a shot. He held her in a bear hug and withstood her struggles and kicks without so much as a grunt as he carried her to the back of the room, which swallowed them both in shadows.

Kat's hands remained pointed at Neal, weaving the strings of light, vibrating them. He was no longer in pain. As she'd promised, it now felt pleasurable, as if he were receiving the best massage of his life.

The Lady lowered her arms. He remained levitating. Not only were his physical senses slightly enhanced, he was more in touch with his intuition. His sixth sense . . .

" . . . I have it, don't I?" he asked. "The Virus . . ."

"The Creator's last laugh at us," Lady Kat said. "Not content to just have our natural desires make us outsiders, the Fool wanted to punish us with what some call a disease. But, Ice and me, we call it a blessing. We *know* it's a blessing."

Ice. Neal remembered why he was here. He remembered Katrisha. He looked toward the back of the room and focused. His eyes converted the ebon shadows into white steam as his sight cut through the murk and he saw the big guy trying to strap the ball-gagged but still-struggling agent to a modified dentist's chair.

Neal unsteadily lowered himself to the floor. Once sure of his footing, he rushed toward them. He stopped when he felt hundreds of icicle-needles sticking his backside, increasing as rapidly in number as in cold-sharp intensity.

"Don't interfere," Kat said. "That betrayer is overdue for her punishment."

All the babble about killing some "One," blessings, and betrayals meant nothing to Neal. He was overwhelmed already by his own personal torture and revelation. And he didn't like what he saw happening with Katrisha. He didn't know or care what exactly was holding him back. He only focused on the big man, glaring at him with all the frustrated anger that had been pooling inside him. He neither blinked nor flinched when a gauzy red overshadowed his vision as his sight telescoped, focusing on the big man's ear.

Ice's head jerked back as if he'd been shot. He recovered and glared at Neal.

"Knotty!" he called. "Let him go! If he wants to try to melt me, let him come up and do it to my face!"

Neal turned around as best he could and saw that the Lady had both hands outstretched. Knotted, parti-colored strings of light that seemed to emanate from her fingertips were attached to his backside. She balled her hands into fists and lowered them, letting him go. Instead of rushing toward Ice as invited, Neal turned fully toward the woman.

"Whatever you are, whatever you're trying to do, to me or who-the-hell-ever, I don't care. But I'm not going to let you hurt my partner. Tell him to let her go."

"He already has."

Neal felt the steel-girder-like arms encircle his waist from behind. Ice didn't take his time as he had with Katrisha; he instead ran toward the back of the room, toward a black curtain, and leapt, making Neal take the brunt of the crash through the window and impact on the vacant parking lot two stories below.

The thick curtain minimized the pain and kept Neal mostly covered. But the wind had been knocked out of him. He was hardly in any shape to react as he saw Rufus and the other Peacemakers converging on the lot, weapons drawn. Ice was already on his feet, grinning. He seemed to be getting darker, blending into the night, in spite of the abundant light from the lot's several lampposts.

Neal's head was the only part of his body left uncovered. Lucky him. Lucky he hadn't cracked it open on the pavement. He wasn't ready to attempt to move his stinging arms and legs, but his eyes were mobile and strong—strong enough to throw a faint red, white, and blue tartan pattern over the entire landscape within his range of vision. As his sight focused ever closer on the square framing Ice, he shifted the lines, made them bolder, sharper, and imagined them carving the skin off of the big bruiser, making him easier to see in the nighttime, shaving off the coal-black, leaving what remained gleaming white.

Ice now appeared as a muscle-bound snowman in a thong, a grotesquerie who didn't stop grinning even after he noticed the change. He seemed to care nothing about the Peacemaker agents surrounding him, lining him up in their sights. He just looked at Neal.

"Man who had a force-field watch now has a skin-shearing stare. You're a natural." Ice pointed his thumb toward some of the agents. "They will love you—if they live through this."

Neal couldn't believe his eyes when he changed Ice's appearance—most of it was accomplished through a subconscious will to both expose and stop him—but what happened next was beyond both his belief and his control.

The man-mountain moved at the speed of an avalanche on fast-forward as he raced from Peacemaker agent to Peacemaker agent, choking them with one hand while smacking them across the face with another. He grinned all the while. The spectacle was perversely reminiscent of a game of freeze tag; as soon as Ice touched an agent, that agent froze in place. Ice managed to touch them all without any of them getting off a shot.

The big man stopped running but kept grinning as he loomed over Neal. His skin seemed embedded with miniscule ice-flakes, each of which glinted and glimmered in the light.

Crystals of some sort actually were embedded in his skin—a step up, Neal guessed, from mere piercings and tattoos. But the sparkles only momentarily held his attention. He was more drawn to something on Ice's arm, a relatively tiny gadget he hadn't noticed before due to there being so much else to notice about the big man.

Ice held up his left wrist. "This little watch of yours has done wonders to enhance my talents. On any other night, I would've just snapped their necks or something."

Neal tried to get to his feet, struggling with the curtain and his own disorientation as he realized the watch's properties may've somehow had a hand in helping protect him during his fall.

Ideally, even now, the prototypical watches were supposed to envelope the wearer in a skintight electromagnetic field that would act as an imperfect force field. Once the necessary adjustments were made after the testing phase, the perfect device would have the ability to warp space and time within the field, make the wearer more agile, give him or her the ability to turn invisible, and bestow many other benefits that could even the odds in a battle with evil—the evil primarily being outlaw Virus-carriers. Those who could, without the aid of any devices, manipulate types of electromagnetic radiation—mostly visible light, infrared radiation, and x-rays. But they were growing more powerful, particularly those Virus-carriers classified by the HSA as "The Infinite Definite." They had honed their abilities to such a degree they were considered less than human and more like supernatural creatures. The terrorists had no leaders, but they operated in pairs, causing mayhem, spreading chaos. Pairs like Ice, and—

"Knotty!" Ice was looking up toward where he'd barreled through the window.

Still dizzy but on his feet, Neal hesitantly turned and looked up.

Lady Kat—*Knotty*—was hovering outside the window. She was holding a flogger in her left hand. A web the color of holly leaves and fruit emanated from her outstretched right hand to fill the space of the broken window. Katrisha's unconscious and naked body was stuck in the middle.

Neal knew it would be futile, but he shouted it anyway. "Let her go!"

Knotty smiled and descended as if riding an invisible elevator. She stopped roughly ten feet from the ground, maybe as far as she could go without losing control of the web. "What would you give for her?"

"Keep the damn watch!" Neal shouted.

"We don't care about your toys," Knotty said. "We have our own."

"Then why did you steal it?"

"I didn't. You left it behind, remember?"

She had him there.

"I was simply going to hold on to it as a keepsake," Knotty said. "But once Ice and I took a closer look at it . . ."

"What the hell do you want from me?" Neal asked.

Knotty gave him a smile that seemed equally seductive and malicious. "I've had my eye on you for a while, agent. You see, Katrisha here is . . . an old friend of mine. And I've been very interested in her attempts to uphold *morality* in light of what she'd been involved with in her past."

Neal knew nothing about it, and wasn't sure he wanted to. Though it was very clear that Katrisha, too, was a Virus-carrier.

"You want your toy back?" Knotty said. "Ice, give it to him."

Ice unfastened the watch from his wrist and tossed it at Neal. It landed somewhere in the folds of the curtain.

"I want Katrisha back," Neal said. "And I want all the other agents released from whatever this thing did to them."

"You may have all that," Knotty said, "in exchange for your help."

"*What?*"

"I long ago sensed you had a latent form of the Virus. And I used a little bit of, shall we say, *sensual* magick to help bring out the best in the worst. Thank my own *black-fantastic* arts, agent. Most people discover they have the Virus when it puts their body through *hell*—seizures, vomiting, mind turned inside out . . . and that's the least of it. You should be licking my stilettos. I made your transition *smooth*."

"Why?" Neal asked. "Why did you do this?"

"During one of our recent . . . *play* sessions, Ice and I happened upon a dirty little secret. *Your* dirty little secret."

Neal shook his head. "My—?"

"Your Agency has a secret unit composed entirely of magick-enhanced Virus-carriers. The chief one—*Violet Valentinus*—has been working on building a prison camp located in another dimension. Your agency thinks he's fully in their employ, but Valentinus believes himself to be an *angel*, an agent of the same Creator who is punishing us, the same Fool who is having a laugh at us. In the service of this Fool, Valentinus has been attacking other Virus-carriers at random. Destroying their bodies and sending their souls to this prison for who knows what reason. Now that you've been turned out, he'll come after you, and probably soon. He's coming after all of us. Unless we stop him."

"I know you," Neal said. "I know your *kind*. You're *ID*. Infinite-Definite terrorists. Why should I believe or trust you?"

"Trust *this*," Ice said. "He's coming here. Tonight."

"Yes," Knotty said. "I've prepared a dark tantric trick that'll ensure he shows. Ice and I have a plan to stop him. With your help, it'll work."

"Why do you need help?" Neal asked with a sneer. "You two are so bad-ass. Why not take him on by yourselves?"

"Valentinus is used to encountering our *kind*, as you put it, in pairs," Knotty said. "Based on our own research, we figure three is his unlucky number."

"Three is a magick number, after all," Ice said.

"Then why did you need me?" Neal asked; then, though he almost hated to say it out loud, "Why not just use Katrisha?"

"We are," Ice said with a chuckle. "As bait. We'll be doing a little ice-fishin' tonight."

"But you," Knotty said to Neal, "you're the type of guy Valentinus goes for. A true sexual misfit. He loves taking *our kind* down."

"We're going to hit him before he hits us," Ice said.

"You help us," Knotty said. "Ice will let your fellow agents go. Unfrozen. *Alive*."

"And what'll you two do then?" Neal asked.

"We'll go on our merry way."

"And Katrisha?"

"That's the best part," Knotty said. "She'll be my special gift to you . . ." There was that mixed-signals smile again. "I remember all you told me during our sweet, *sweet* time together this morning."

Neal briefly averted his gaze. He was well past the point of blushing, but her words still hit a soft spot.

"You help us," Knotty said, "you get her—in whatever condition you want her. Obedient. Totally compliant. All yours, mind and body. Willing to serve all your imaginable desires . . ."

Neal could no longer stand to look at the twisted expressions on Knotty's face. He turned his attention to Ice but saw the same damn thing. They and their words were beyond distasteful—but . . .

He wondered if Rufus and the others, despite their frozen state, could see and hear what was happening. None of them had moved an inch since Ice had tagged them. And, Katrisha . . . Was she conscious, or was she taking all of this in? What were all of them thinking of Neal? He was their only potential knight—a knight in no armor. He was the reason they were here in the first place. He was the reason the whole force had been taken out by a couple of deviants. He, another deviant.

HSA briefings on Infinite-Definite associates had always portrayed them as light-manipulating zombies, diseased and mostly mindless terrorists, bent on spreading chaos and confusion until the world exploded. These two certainly weren't mindless. But were they crazy? He didn't know anything of the secret agent they mentioned—this *Violet Valentinus*. But they seemed hell-bent on conjuring and killing him. And if he helped them . . . Well, even if Katrisha weren't unconscious, he could always attempt to make the case he was being coerced. After all, he was. He was bargaining for the life of his fellow agents. He had no other out—for, undoubtedly, if he refused to help them, he'd be killed, as would every other agent on site.

"Choose now, agent," Knotty said. "Our window is growing smaller."

Their window. Neal gazed at Katrisha's nude, splayed body as he thought of Knotty's promise. Promises could be broken, and refused, but . . .

"Okay," he said with a sigh. "What do you need me to do?"

"We made some adjustments to your gadget," Ice said. "Put it on."

Neal had no choice but to drop the curtain and totally reveal his nakedness as he went through the folds to retrieve the watch. After he found and fastened it, his hand's skin color immediately changed. One finger black with ice-white nail, another finger white with coal-black nail, a white-and-black checkered pattern across his hand, up his arm . . . "The fu—" He gaped while his skin color changed in a pattern that seemed both haphazard and meticulously planned until he was totally black and white.

"A safeguard," Knotty said. "An offense as well as armor against the one who is coming. Ice and I have our own. Now, get ready."

He was a naked chessboard, one upon which no queen would ever tread. At this point, he wasn't sure what "ready" meant.

"Watch for any fluctuations in the air," Knotty said. "When he appears, look at him—*hard*—let your new sense take over. Ice and I will do the rest."

Neal noticed Ice's skin color had not changed back to black. His new abilities were a mystery to him. He knew vaguely he could manipulate light—but changing someone's skin pigment? Embedded crystals or no embedded crystals, had Neal actually done that to Ice, or had that just been Ice's reaction to something else Neal was intuitively trying to do? Hell, would intuition be enough against this Valentinus?

Knotty had ascended back up to the second floor. She was eye-level with Katrisha and speaking something that sounded like melodic gibberish. A lot of random, rhyming words. Watching and listening, Neal realized for the first time the knotty similarity between the names Lady *Kat* and *Kat*risha. How coincidental was that?

The web vibrated and glowed even brighter as Knotty moved closer to her captive. Katrisha's body trembled, appearing to experience the same frisson Neal accomplished after a successful session of auto-eroticism. Knotty brought her face closer to hers, her lips closer to hers.

"What is she doing?" Neal asked.

"It's just magick," Ice said. "Nothing you need to worry about."

Knotty finally stopped speaking in tongues and kissed the woman, using lips and tongue while keeping her eyes wide open. The web vibrated even more violently as visible waves of violet electricity seemed to emanate along the strands, outward from the center.

Neal didn't want to look away, but he sensed something happening somewhere above him. He tilted his head upward and saw a patch of shimmering air high up in the sky. The shimmer became an electric-blue tear, and through it flew a large, screeching eagle seemingly composed entirely of violet light.

The frozen Peacemaker agents collapsed as Ice ran to a far corner of the lot. Neal figured he'd had to concentrate at least a little to keep them in place, but now that the big game was here, Ice had to shift all of his focus, letting his previous victims sleep. At least Neal hoped they were sleeping.

The screeching eagle dove straight for Knotty. The woman certainly was a professional . . . *something*. She maintained the web as she whipped her flogger toward the eagle, forcing it to rapidly molt most of the feathers of light from its body. They fell like fiery confetti but burned out quickly. The wings on its back were unaffected but the thing slowed as its body resolved itself into a man's—a giant, nude man with a head shaped like some kind of wolf.

Valentinus.

Now at a closer range than his initial appearance, his body appeared at least eight feet in length, but the wings of violet fire spanned at least twice as wide.

Valentinus had slowed his progression toward Knotty but didn't stop as he closed the distance—roughly forty feet, thirty feet, fifteen feet—until Knotty suddenly stopped flogging with her left hand and swung her right.

The entire web, Katrisha included, flung toward the winged thing. Valentinus was unable to swerve or stop as Katrisha's body involuntarily embraced him and the web of honey-colored light enwrapped them both.

Valentinus's wings snuffed out, but the embracing two hung in the air long enough for Ice—who'd begun running when the web was tossed—to make an astounding leap at the two and rapidly slap his hands on several parts of both bodies before dropping again.

Katrisha and Valentinus slowed in their descent, until Ice made another run-and-touch, and then another. The big man moved like an Olympic sprinter, or maybe more like an Olympic skier, one used to taking to the air and flipping, maneuvering with ease. When Ice was done, the embracing two descended no more. They hung as if in suspended animation inside a transparent cocoon.

"Now, agent!" Knotty yelled. "Gaze at them! Think! Concentrate! *Glaze* them!"

Neal gazed at the target, but he wasn't sure what to think. Katrisha had her arms wrapped around a giant man who had the head of a wolf. Both were naked. Both were seemingly asleep. It was like something out of an exceedingly perverse fairy tale.

"Stare in *anger*," Knotty said. "Remember what I told you he *is*. Remember what *you* told *me* this morning.

Neal continued to stare, and started to remember. He'd told Knotty about the lack of intimacy in his life, and his desire to have a child. And now he was looking at . . .

Knotty. She'd set up this pose. On purpose. To humiliate him. To *trick* him. Knotty and Ice had set him up to take out not only their enemy but his own partner as well. As if he hadn't already dug himself into enough trouble today.

Knotty met his eyes. She seemed to know what he was thinking. She turned toward the open window, preparing— Neal assumed—to whisk herself back into her playpen for cover.

He wasn't as stupid as he looked.

He focused on her head and thought of fireworks, bursting in a splendid array of colors. He soon heard the screams that often accompanied such a display, but they were all coming from Knotty, whose hair was popping and crackling and blazing like wiry sparklers.

She fell backward in an arc toward the ground. Ice raced to her rescue. Neal focused on his skin and played connect the dots with the embedded crystals, those crystals that twinkled like stars.

Ice hollered and fell on his face, shrieking, as fires the size of match heads flared up all over his body. He rolled on the ground until—small miracle—Knotty crash landed on top of him.

Both appeared to be unconscious. Neither was burning anymore—most likely because Neal stopped focusing on either one. His attention drifted upward.

Valentinus was awake and ensured that any who might be looking believed it by flaring his violet eagle's wings at a span that seemed a mile long. He descended, cradling Katrisha's body in his arms as he landed just a few feet in front of Neal.

Neal didn't move. He may've been in awe. He may've been scared. Or he may've just been too exhausted. He wasn't entirely sure, but he stood his ground as Valentinus approached.

Neal gazed as the wolf's head shapeshifted into a man's. His body had an odd skin tone. Vanilla glazed with violet. As Valentinus neared, more and more visible light—*cold fire*—gathered about that strangely hued body, waves of violet, indigo, and blue that shrouded most of him like a philosopher's robe. The wings still flared behind him, but they'd been greatly reduced in size. Neal wondered why he wasn't blinded by the whole spectacle as he gazed at it. He guessed it was an effect of his new condition.

Valentinus stopped a few paces in front of him. Neal looked up into those deep purple eyes. The angel really was about eight feet tall.

"Take her." The angel appropriately spoke with a voice that, in Neal's ears at least, pealed like thunder.

Neal allowed him to lay Katrisha's body in his arms. He looked down into her face. She did not appear to be breathing.

Valentinus stepped backward and leaped several dozen feet into the air, flipped, and landed next to Knotty and Ice.

He picked the latter up by his throat, lifted him off the ground, and said something Neal couldn't understand.

Ice regained consciousness and began to struggle. Valentinus thrust his free hand into Ice's chest, as if he really were made of snow, and ripped out a bloody lump that could've only been his heart. The blood glistened as streams of light flowed from Valentinus's eyes and mouth into Ice's. The latter's body disintegrated as if it had been reduced to shaved ice.

Perhaps it really had. The mass on the ground seemed to melt away as Knotty stirred.

More alert than she initially appeared, Knotty lunged at Valentinus the moment she saw him. He grabbed her by the throat and gave her the same treatment as her partner. Her skin darkened and sunk in on itself until he let her go. She disintegrated into a pile of ashes.

Valentinus met Neal's eyes. This time, the agent was ready to run away, but having Katrisha in his arms would've made it difficult. It wouldn't have mattered anyway. The angel closed the distance between them in a blink. He loomed over Neal, staring down into his eyes.

"Guess it's my turn now," Neal said with a sigh.

"It would have been," Valentinus thundered, "if you had actually allowed yourself to be tricked by them."

Relief delivered in a way that was not at all comforting. Neal shouldn't have expected anything less at this point. "They said *this*—the pattern of my skin, my watch—it would all protect me from you."

"And you believed them," Valentinus said. "I suppose they did not have IQ tests for Heartland Security agents when you joined."

And there was the insult he was expecting.

"They were simply mocking you," Valentinus said.

"And me. Your abilities have been slightly enhanced due to that piece of technology, but you would have not been able to stop me."

"Stop you from taking me to some kind of extra-dimensional prison," Neal said. "A lockup for sexual *weirds*. Did they lie about that, too?"

Valentinus didn't answer right away. His eyes flashed as he broke eye contact with Neal, looking him up and down, before responding. "Their souls are now in an extra-dimensional realm under my supervision. They will not be able to escape or harm anyone ever again. The two mockers, they turned your skin into a mockery of a prisoner's uniform from years past. They had no intention that you would be saved. You were to suffer the same fate as them, or go in their place."

"Why?"

"They were dangerous thrill seekers, like all the other two-person cells of The Infinite Definite. *Errorists*. These two, unlike many others, were proficient in various forms of dirty but powerful magick. I came after them several days ago, and failed. Since then, their Modus Operandi has been to seduce the naïve into going along with their plans to destroy me. Each time, after drawing me out and attacking, and realizing their latest plan will not work, they fled, leaving the seduced to face my wrath. This was their third attempt, and their last."

"Katrisha . . ." Neal looked at the woman in his arms. "The other agents . . . Are they dead? They've been out for a while. Katrisha isn't breathing."

"They are in an altered state. Neither dead nor alive at the moment. But I will take care of them."

The angel's last sentence was a little too cryptic for Neal. He practically blurted, "Are you really on our side?" he asked. "The HSA, I mean. Are you one of our agents?"

"I am an agent of One yet to be born. One who will set right all that seems imperfect in this world, all that is odd in the sight of its inhabitants."

Still a bit too cryptic for Neal, but what else should he expect from an angel? "What now?" he asked, hoping for something a little more straightforward.

The angel's eyes blazed before he said, "I can let you live the rest of your days on this Earth as you are now, or I can offer you a release."

If those were his two choices, the answer was obvious, but "What do you mean by 'release'?" Neal had been with enough escorts to fear the answer.

"I can send your soul to where the Errorists have gone," Valentinus said.

Neal had a clear response to that.

"Or," Valentinus said, "I can give a new role. A redeeming role."

The crypticism had crept back—but, really, what were his other options?

"Make the same offer to Katrisha," Neal said. "After everything that's happened tonight, I doubt she can go back to the Agency. I doubt she wants to. But what do I know? She deserves to make an informed decision."

"And your decision?"

Neal sighed. "The new role, I guess."

"Lay the woman down, gently."

Neal turned to his left, walked a few paces, and did as instructed. Straightening, he again made eye contact with the angel.

"Every creature living today was born imperfect," Valentinus said as he moved a step closer, "with a defect. Some poets might call it a necessary flaw in the constitution of a creature. And it is necessary, once recognized, for one to embrace and overcome it on the way to perfection. Sacrifice the chunk of ice in oneself to become a being suffused with the passion of eternal fire."

Valentinus thrust his right hand into Neal's chest. Neal didn't have a chance to flinch, let alone move as the fingers clutched his heart and his body shuddered with an ice-cold frisson.

Valentinus retracted his hand as quickly as he'd thrust it forward. The last thing Neal saw was the angel holding up a fiery lump in front of his face, which had melted into a skull with eyes and mouth filled with violet flames.

NEAL STOOD IN A WIDE, seven-walled room made entirely of glass, or something that approximated glass. The walls and ceiling gave view to a fathomless green-bluish haze populated with black phantomlike streaks. The room somehow existed simultaneously on Earth and outside of the known universe. It was a meeting room. A planning room.

To Neal's right was a man who could create and remotely control holographic facsimiles of himself. To Neal's left was a woman whose every word came out as a flying insect of light, each one ready to sting or bite. And behind him were three others with varying abilities that had some connection to light and sound.

And Neal—he was the one who could, among other magick tricks, generate limited-range force fields and cast expertly woven nets of light with his eyes or fingers, nets that could freeze, burn, and do other cruel things to evildoers.

He and the rest were all listening to a briefing by the Equinox, a more-than-ten-foot-tall man-creature who had talons for hands, cloven hooves for feet, and a unicorn's head. Heaven knows what all he could do; Neal had only been told that he could transmute matter into energy.

The Equinox was a "consultant"—from where exactly Neal wasn't privy to know. The rest of the room's occupants served in the black ops group known as the Dark Artzmen, or those who wore—quite literally—parts of their own souls as skin. The whole operation was the pet project of an HSA official in Washington, a wise man with *magickal* connections. A man who believed the real-deal Apocalypse was coming and was doing everything he could to stop it. In light of everything that was transpiring on the Earth these days, the Artzmen group was quite a creative idea.

Katrisha had opted to stay with the Agency's branch in Indiana. She would no doubt be viewed very differently now that they knew she had the Virus, but she was in no danger of losing her job. In fact, Neal wouldn't be surprised if they promoted her. After all, the Agency needed all the help it could get.

The Equinox was briefing him and the others on a mission they were to undertake immediately. Gargantuan creatures were appearing in the far reaches of the globe. Some of them seemed to materialize out of thin air, others seemed to crawl out of the oceans. The Artzmen had to take them down as quickly and efficiently as possible.

Outside the walls, out in what Neal called the "ether," something that appeared like violet ball lighting bounced and streaked, raggedly zigzagged from one spot to another before blinking out altogether. *Valentinus*—off on another mission. Though he was the chief Artzman, he often worked independently on projects secret even to the rest of them. Whatever he did, he did it quickly. Rumors abounded that he operated in multiple places at once.

Neal owed him a lot. Valentinus had given his physiology a little extra tweaking, which served to enhance his innate abilities even more. So long as he stuck to the regimen required by the Artzmen, he would go far. Valentinus had also given him some words of wisdom: "Love is not about sex. Or friendship. Or companionship. It goes deeper. It's about *Creation*."

Neal had a purpose, and a place. He was no angel, not even a saint. He was more like a fighting monk, celibate and separated from humankind but dedicated to a singular, creative idea.

Finally, a suitable position.

ABOUT THE SERIES

When their bodies are overwhelmed by an onslaught of parasites that feed on blood and light, most victims of the White Fire Virus die quickly but in excruciating pain. They could be considered the lucky ones. Those who survive continue to live on in physical and psychological torment; they also find themselves endowed with a range of supernatural abilities. Many of these survivors consider themselves angels, potential saviors of humanity. Others want nothing less than the death of God. And there are a few who are even more ambitious.

Eve of Light is a dark metaphysical fantasy—philosophical, intense, action-packed, and *surreal*.

The Core Novels
BloodLight: The Apocalypse of Robert Goldner
Broken Angels (Eve of Light, Book I)
Divinities, Entangled (Eve of Light, Book II)

The Deviant-Hunter Stories
Deviant-Hunter: Blood Oath
Deviant-Hunter, Killer of Saints
Deviant-Hunter's Sabbath

Other Stories on the Fringe
The Lark

Heaven's Gun
Rogue Beauty
FoolKillers
Knotty & Ice
Influx

EVE OF LIGHT STORY ORDER

Although it is recommended that readers begin the series with either a standalone story or *Broken Angels*, there is no suggested reading order. What follows, however, is a list of where the current stories generally fall within the timeline of events.

The Lark
BloodLight: The Apocalypse of Robert Goldner
Heaven's Gun
Rogue Beauty
Deviant-Hunter: Blood Oath
Deviant-Hunter, Killer of Saints
Deviant-Hunter's Sabbath
Broken Angels (Eve of Light, Book I)
FoolKillers
Knotty & Ice
Divinities, Entangled (Eve of Light, Book II)
Influx

ABOUT THE AUTHOR

Harambee K. Grey-Sun is the author of several novels, novellas, and short stories, including *Hero Zero, Colder Than Ice,* and *Unfair Play.* For more information about his books and ongoing projects, please visit www.harambee-greysun.com.

For more information:

Click Here for Author's Website
www.harambeegreysun.com

ALSO BY HARAMBEE K. GREY-SUN

BY HARAMBEE GREY-SUN

Poetry

Spring's Fall (Autumn Numbers * Book I)

Wine Songs, Vinegar Verses

Trinity & Its Twin